THOMAS the TOADilly Terrible Bully

Written by
Janice Levy

Illustrated by
Bill Slavin and **Esperança Melo**

Eerdmans Books for Young Readers
Grand Rapids, Michigan • Cambridge, U.K.

To Rick, with all my love.
— *J.L.*

To our good friend Bonnie.
— *B.S. and E.M.*

Text © 2014 Janice Levy
Illustrations © 2014 Bill Slavin and Esperança Melo

Published in 2014 by Eerdmans Books for Young Readers,
an imprint of Wm. B. Eerdmans Publishing Co.
2140 Oak Industrial Dr. NE
Grand Rapids, Michigan 49505
P.O. Box 163, Cambridge CB3 9PU U.K.

www.eerdmans.com/youngreaders

Manufactured at Tien Wah Press
in Malaysia in July 2013, first printing

20 19 18 17 16 15 14   9 8 7 6 5 4 3 2 1

Library of Congress Cataloging-in-Publication Data

Levy, Janice.
Thomas the toadilly terrible bully / by Janice Levy; Illustrated by Bill Slavin and Esperança Melo.
pages cm
Summary: After moving to a new town and feeling ignored, a young toad tries to act like a bully,
but learns the value of being a good friend instead.
ISBN 978-0-8028-5373-8
[1. Bullying — Fiction. 2. Friendship — Fiction. 3. Toads — Fiction.]
I. Slavin, Bill, illustrator. II. Melo, Esperança, illustrator. III. Title.
PZ7.L5832Th 2014
[E] — dc23
2013024834

The illustrations were created with acrylics on gessoed paper.
The display and text type was set in Green Plain.

Thomas was new in town.

He dressed to impress. He strutted his stuff.

He got in everyone's face.

"Chill," said the other toads.

But Thomas didn't. He hated being ignored.

"If I can't make friends," he thought,
"I'll be a bully instead."

But Thomas was an awful bully.

*Toad*illy terrible.

He couldn't push anyone around.

His abs were flabby.

His voice squeaked.

HICCUP!

Hopping too high
made him hiccup.

Even crickets gave
him the creeps.

"Move it or lose it!" he ordered. "I'm bad-to-the-bone!"
But the other toads just giggled. "You couldn't hurt a fly."

Thomas sulked.

He *really* hated being ignored.

So he practiced his moves.

He rehearsed his lines
in the shower.

But his jokes weren't mean enough.

His faces weren't scary enough.

He just couldn't pull it off.

"There must be someone I can push around," Thomas thought.

He decided to lie low . . .

. . . until he saw Gomer.

Thomas pounced.

He crossed his eyes and spit.

"Ptooey," he croaked. "Your mama has bug breath!"

Gomer buried his head. He began to cry.

Thomas puffed out his chest. "Am I bad-to-the-bone or what? I *toad*illy ruined your day."

"It's not your fault," Gomer said.

"Oh yeah?" snapped Thomas. "Says who?"

Thomas turned. *There* was the baddest-to-the-bone bully he'd ever seen.

"He's been after me all day," Gomer whispered.

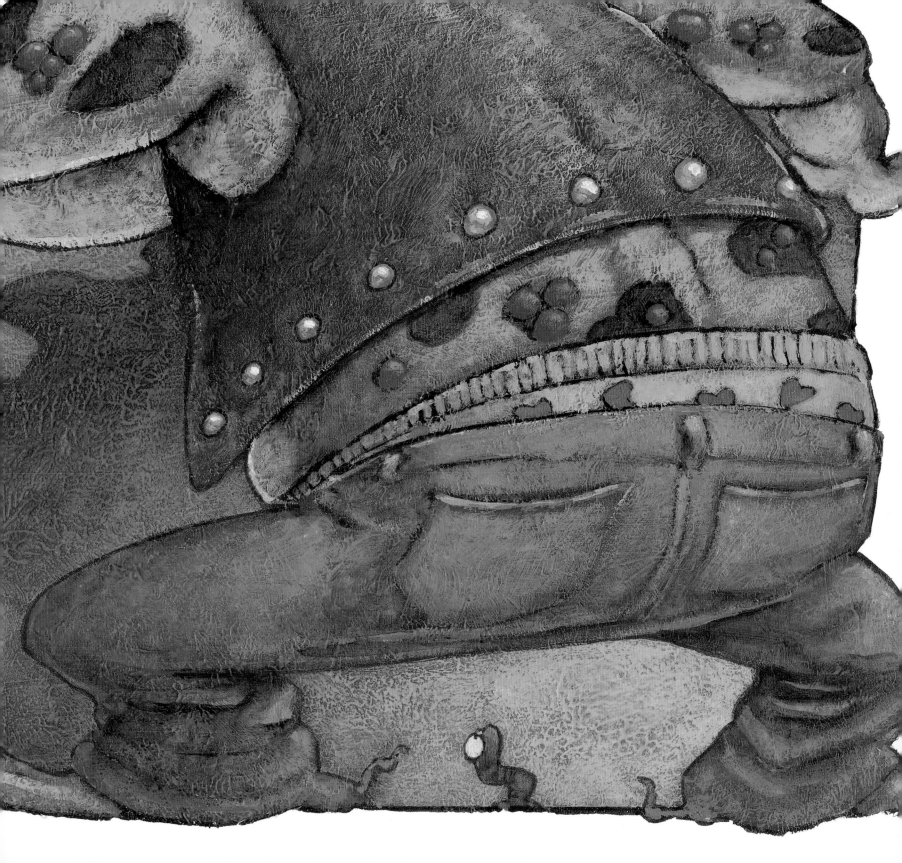

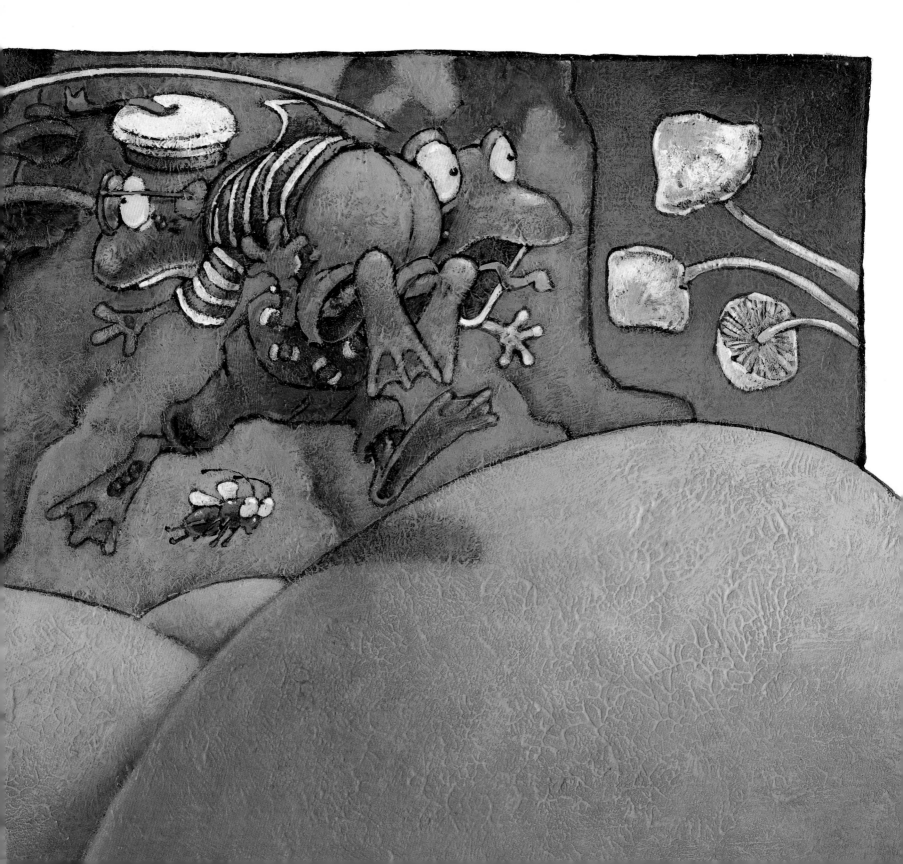

Soon the bully had them cornered.

"P-p-pick on someone your own size," Thomas said.

"There isn't anybody my own size," he snorted. "I eat tadpoles like you for breakfast!"

Thomas thought fast. He threw a rock into the pond. "Well, the bully in the pond eats rocks for breakfast."

The bully bent over. He saw the baddest-to-the-bone bully he'd ever seen.

"RRRRBIT!" he said. "This pond isn't big enough for the two of us!"

And with that, he jumped in.

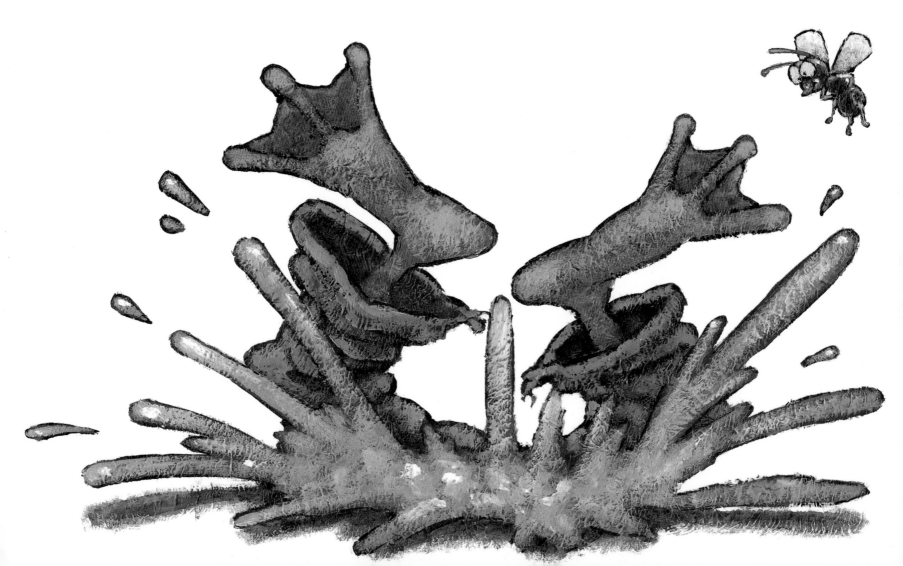

Thomas and Gomer hurried away. They dried off in the sun and shared some snacks.

"I'm a *toad*illy terrible bully," Thomas sighed.

Gomer smiled. "But you're a *toad*illy terrific friend."